THE STORM BOOK

The Storm

Story by Charlotte Zolotow

HarperTrophy
A Division of HarperCollinsPublishers

Book

Pictures by Margaret Bloy Graham

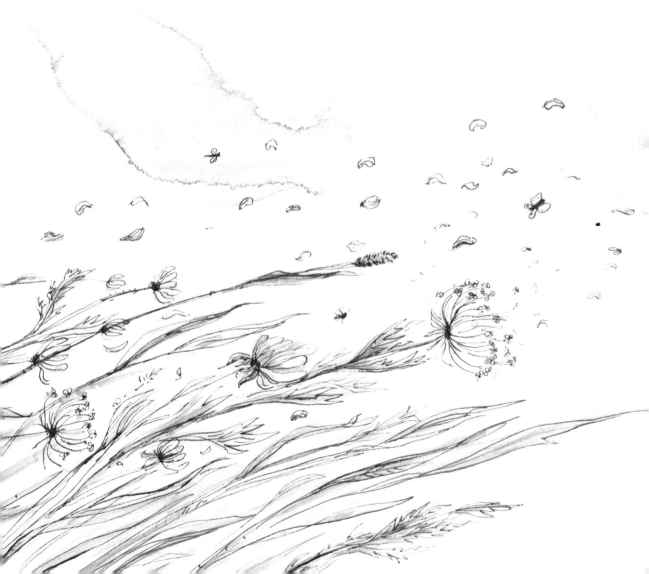

To

Dr. Eugene Eisner,

who knows the child in

each of us

THE STORM BOOK

Text copyright 1952 by Charlotte Shapiro Zolotow
Text copyright renewed 1980 by Charlotte Zolotow
Illustrations copyright 1952 by Margaret Bloy Graham
Illustrations copyright renewed 1980 by Margaret Bloy Graham
Printed in Mexico.
All rights in this book are reserved.
Library of Congress catalog card number: 52-7880
ISBN 0-06-027025-X
ISBN 0-06-027026-8 (lib. bdg.)
ISBN 0-06-443194-0 (pbk.)

IT IS a day in the country, and everything is hot. The grass looks dry and parched. The buttercups are sticky with dust; the daisies' white petals look gray; and all the flowers, the rambler roses climbing up the gate, the hollyhocks leaning against the house, hang limply on their stems.

The little boy can almost see the heat quivering up like mist from the earth. A little caterpillar climbs carefully up a dusty blade of grass and then climbs down again. There is a special hot stillness over everything. The white fox terrier has crawled under the latticework of the porch and lies sleeping in the shade. Even the birds seem too hot to sing, for there is not a sound among the leaves.

But the hazy sky begins to shift, and the yellow heat turns gray. Everything is the same color—one enormous listless gray world where not a breath stirs and the birds don't sing. There isn't the slightest motion of a branch, the slightest whisper of a breeze. And still there is something expectant in the growing darkness; something is astir, something soundless and still for which the little boy waits.

He waits and he sees dark clouds beginning to form, throwing their shadow over the parched fields, moving one after another until they cover the sky and the world is black as night. A little cool wind suddenly races through the trees, sways the rambler roses, bends the daisies and buttercups and Queen Anne's lace and the long grass until they make a great silver sighing stretch down the hill.

Then it happens! Shooting through the sky like a streak of starlight comes a flash so beautiful, so fast, that the little boy barely has time to see the flowers straining into the storm wind.

"Oh, Mother," he calls, *"what was that?"*

"Lightning," his mother answers, "that our own lamplight comes from." The little boy thinks of the lamp in his room, with its warm golden glow. And he thinks of the lightning flashing through the sky. The lightning was like a wild white wolf running free in the woods and the lamp like the gentle white terrier who came when the little boy called.

And now from somewhere beyond the hill comes the great rolling rrrrrrrrrrrmmmmmmmmmmmmm-mmmmDDDDDDDDDDDDDDDRRRR R R R R of the thunder.

"What's that?" the little boy shouts.

"Rain clouds breaking against each other, and that is the sound they make," his mother says. Now there is a silence again in the dark world, stillness, and then the whole sky lights up in one blinding starry flash of lightning.

The sky darkens again as the thunder draws closer, rolling loudly nearer, until, with a sudden explosion, it crashes overhead and a silver torrent of rain slants down. The daisies bend almost to the ground under the tearing weight of the wind and the rain sweeping over the rambler roses and trees, as they toss in the cool huge arms of the storm.

Miles away in the storm-darkened city, a young man closes his book and gets up to look out of the window. Below him on the street, the lighted store windows shine on the wet sidewalks and every flash of lightning shows people running by, newspapers over their heads or umbrellas held down in front of them to buffet the wind and the rain.

The tops of the tall buildings look cut off by the storm darkness, and the little city trees strain at their roots in their loop-fenced circles, and the wind whips the leaves from their branches. The automobile tires make a swish-swishing sound as they pass.

At the seashore an old fisherman stands boot-deep in the waves, and the wind and rain splatter against his oilskin with a terrible beating sound. His face is wet with sea spray and rain. When the thunder roars, nothing else can be heard, not the wild splashing of the black waves, nor the drive of the rain against the oilskin. It seems as though there is nothing in the world but the tremendous ear-splitting rrrrrMMM-MMMMDDDDDDDRRRRRR R R R of the thunder, followed by streak after streak of cloud-rending light.

Once when the lightning flashes a little brown sandpiper skids across the sand on his way home, so swiftly that he is gone before the light leaves the sky.

In the mountains the rain comes down like a waterfall. Each crash of thunder sounds as though the rocks of the mountains were splitting apart, but each flash of lightning shows them solid and quiet against the sky.

A young husband herds his sheep to shelter. His wife looks out of the window at the storm-torn hills, while their baby sleeps quietly in her arms.

The rain drives against the windows of the little boy's house. It beats a loud tattooing pitpatpitpatting on the roof, and the wind rising and falling in the trees sounds like the sea breaking against the shore.

Slowly the storm subsides. The sky begins to brighten, the thunder rolls away, and only from far, far off now can the little boy hear the rrrrrmmmm-ddddrrrrr, as the wind blows the great clouds away from the cool wet land. The loud pitpatpitting on the roof grows softer, and softer, and slowly becomes a dull pit-a-pat, pit-pit-pit, and at last stops altogether. The air is clean and fresh, and smells of wet earth and growing things.

The rambler roses have covered the ground with a shower of wind-driven sweet-smelling petals. The daisies are still bent from the weight of the rain, and their moist white petals cling together. But already the buttercups are standing straight, fresh and glistening, with one clear raindrop cupped in each shiny yellow blossom.

A queer yellow light spreads over the earth now, so faint, so fine, so beautiful that the little boy lets out his breath with a soft whistling sound. And suddenly all the birds break into song. The glistening wet trees are loud with sharp quick twitterings and long full-noted calls.

Here and there in the sparkling grass a quick brown sparrow pecks around looking for worms. The light covers everything now, the house, the hollyhocks, the great stretch of grass, the trees, and the fresh cool face of the little boy who stands in the doorway watching.

"What's *that!*" he suddenly calls to his mother. She comes to the door and looks through the yellow light to a great curving misty arch of color that, coming from farther than they can see, bends across the sky, over the city; over the yellow storm-whipped sand; over the clean-smelling, bird-singing mountains; over the hill toward the little boy's door.